199531

Published by

SMARTINBOOKS®
P. O. Box 729
Paducah, Kentucky 42002-0729

www.smartinbooks.com
www.hunkerdownbooks.com

In The Garden

ISBN 0-9761765-4-8

FOR MY MOTHER,
Kate Martin.

She loves a garden.

In The Garden

Written and Illustrated

by

Herbert Martin

A SMARTINBOOKS Publication
Paducah, KY 42002-0729

*E*arly in the morning, a little girl leaped from her bed and raced into her flower garden to watch as the day lilies unfolded to greet the sun. Anne smiled because she was eager to work in the garden. What a happy day!

What fun to select the garden spot and plant the seeds in eager anticipation of the magic which nature would provide as the sun and rain and time did their work. Her greatest delight was in keeping it neat and well trimmed by loosening the soil around the plants and pulling the occasional uninvited weed that came to visit.

She loved the beauty; and just as she was in her garden, her garden was also in her.

$\mathcal{A}$nne sipped a cup of the rose petal tea which she had brewed for herself and for the rabbits, turtles, and squirrels who lived there in the garden.

"I really don't like the taste of the tea very much," she said to one particularly friendly rabbit named Other, "but enough sugar in anything will make it seem sweet. You seem to like the carrots we planted along the edge of the garden. They are quite tasty, don't you think?" Other munched on a carrot and appeared to nod.

Not put off by his lack of chattiness, she continued, "What I like most about the roses is how sweet they smell."

She stood, walked over to the roses, smelled the sweet fragrance of one beautiful blossom, and then visited an equally sweet-smelling honeysuckle bush that grew around the base of a nearby oak tree. The scent reached her senses even before she bent over to enjoy it.

"My garden looks pretty," Anne said, "and even the nubby sweet violets feel wonderfully soft when I touch their leaves. I can smell the flowers. I can taste the tea rose. I wish that I could hear them also; I imagine that would be a wonderful sound."

As she spoke, Other was busy being lazy among the tulips and, as expected, ignored her musing. Besides, most times, although he was great company, he was not a very talkative rabbit. He mostly ate carrots and nodded in agreement whenever Anne said something.

Anne, Other, another rabbit, and other animals in the garden all understood each other, and at times, conversation seemed unnecessary. This was especially so at nightfall, when, sadly, the beautiful day lilies had to leave.

Like the sun, the day lily, strong and colorful, blossomed in the morning, grew in brilliance as the daylight shifted shades and measured time in shadows, and then it faded and folded at nightfall. Beauty passes, and even though new blossoms always replaced the old, Anne nonetheless now looked wistfully at the withered remnants of yesterday's glory. Some were lying lifelessly on the ground; others were simply dried shells of lost beauty still standing as stoic tribute to former grandeur.

But today was a new day, and new beautiful day lilies were blooming, bright and brilliantly orange. Anne's friend, Obi, came over to help her enjoy the flowers. The flowers looked happy, and that made the girls happy.

One particularly beautiful blossom attracted Obi's attention. "It's so perfect," she said, "I think we ought to call it 'Dusksun' because its color matches the evening sun."

Anne agreed.

The girls sometimes ran and other times walked through the garden, stopping often to study the beauty of all of Anne's blossoms – the gentle curving of the delicate petals, the soft puffiness of the anther and reed-like filament, the elegance of the pistil with its sticky stigma. Anne imagined herself a bee as she zoomed in closer to study this finery of nature. Other remained faithfully with them, hopping from plant to plant, examining everything.

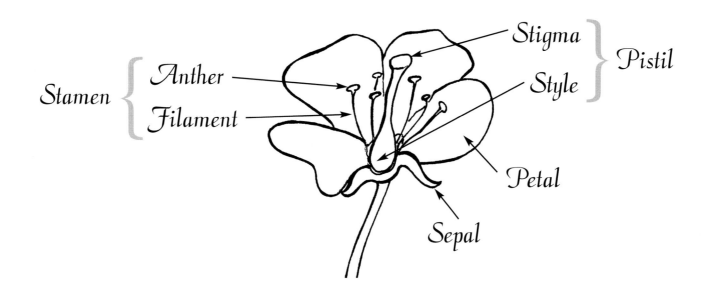

During the day, even more school friends came to visit. Anne looked at her friends, Yuri, Markie, and Pedro, and thought of all the flowers in her garden…

…of the tulips and marigolds and pansies…

…of daffodils and irises…

…of peonies and petunias and poppies…

… and of tiger lilies. Many colors, many shapes; one garden, all flowers.

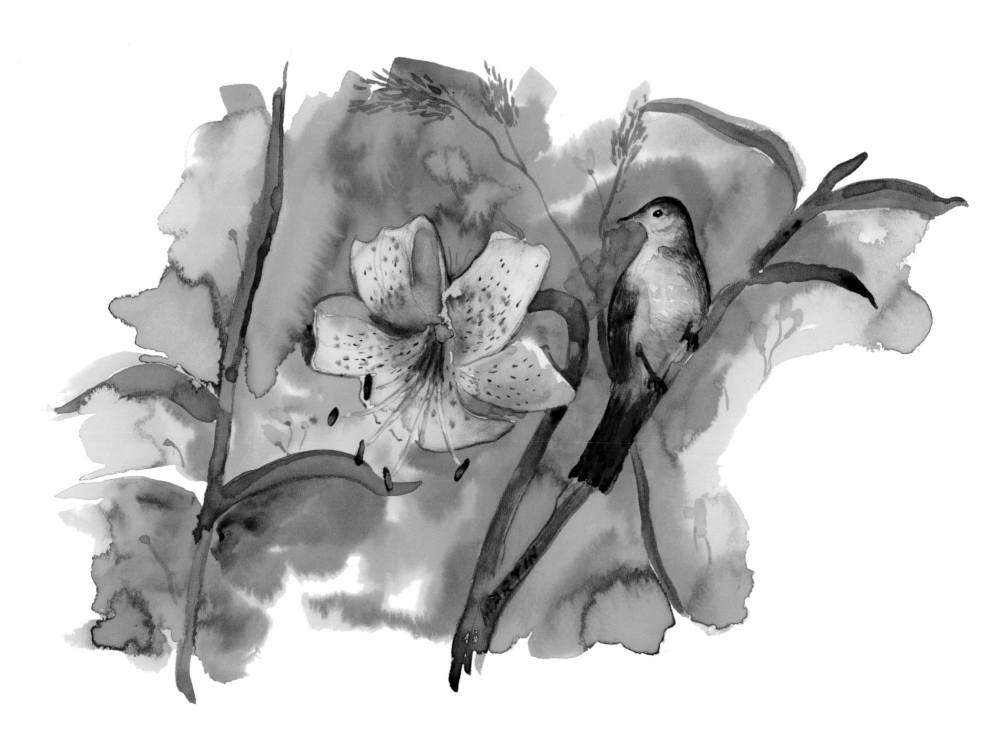

But now was not the time for thought; it was the time for wild, boisterous play,

as magical, fantastic, fun-filled hours sped swiftly past.

Even a brief shower could not dampen the lively spirits of the children. During "Hide and Seek", Anne hid near Dusksun so that she could look at her beautiful, special flower. She grew more and more attached to it as they played, and they played all day. They played so loudly that even the sounds of the birds seemed to mimic their laughter, as the songs of mockingbirds, nightingales, and myna birds are sometimes known to do.

*L*ater in the day, Yuri, Markie, Pedro, Obi, and the rest of her friends left to go home. When it was almost time for her to go into the house and prepare for bed, a great sadness came over Anne because she looked at Dusksun and knew that he would be gone by morning. As she looked through the silence of the evening air at her day lily, a large tear welled up in her eye, trickled down her cheek and landed on one of Dusksun's petals. Just as she was wiping her cheek, she heard a voice speaking from nearby.

"There's no need to cry." It was Other hopping closer to be by her side. "Dusksun will be all right."

They sat down to look at the flower, which now matched the glow of the setting sun. "In nature, beauty is never lost," he said, "It may leave for a time and come back changed, but somehow, beauty lives on forever. Watch from your window tonight. You will see." With that, Other hopped away and disappeared into the evening.

That night, when all was quiet and the moon was bright, Anne went to her window and stared out onto her silver garden. A moonbeam shone brightly down upon Dusksun, and although the once beautiful flower had now withered and was rapidly leaving, it still absorbed the moonlight glimmer and seemed to glow. Anne could easily see it from her bedroom perch. But she was perplexed. What had Other meant to say? What was going to happen?

Anne slipped out of the house and went down to the garden to take a closer look at her flower. She didn't know if the light coming from Dusksun was truly an inner glow or was simply being caused by the bright moonbeam. Anne sat down close by the flower, but she still couldn't tell. She stayed for a little while longer but then went back to her room again to watch from the window.

The night slipped quietly by, and even though an occasional cloud passing overhead temporarily darkened the moon, her little day lily seemed to continue glowing and blinking in the darkness. And still the time passed slowly.

Then gradually something amazing began to happen! The little faded flower started to blink more rapidly – a constant pulsing glow. And as all of its withered petals gently folded and closed completely into lifelessness, Dusksun glimmered and shimmered in place and became lighter, more airy than ever before – a delicate, feathery weightlessness. Slowly, effortlessly, like warm air rising, it drifted up, up into the trees and disappeared. For a while, Anne sat transfixed, and she watched and listened. She knew that something had happened, but she didn't know exactly what.

And then it came to her – softly at first but then more loudly and more easily heard. It was like a song – gentle, sweet music. Beauty had taken a different form, and from the spot in the trees where Dusksun, the day lily, had vanished, Anne heard a melody. She heard the first song of a nightingale.

The next morning, the sun again rose over the beautiful garden. And, once again, Anne was happy because there was joy in the garden. It was a happy day.

THE END.

In The Garden

Text and Illustrations ©2005 by Herbert Martin
Published in Paducah, Kentucky

Printed in Korea

Thanks to Adrienne Mundy, Tracy Jordan, Cathy Glisson and to Karie Fritts.